The CATERPILLAR
and the POLLIWOG

Jack Kent

Prentice-Hall, Inc. - Englewood Cliffs, N. J.

To John Igo

Printed in the United States of America   · J
Prentice-Hall International, Inc., London
Prentice-Hall of Australia, Pty. Ltd., Sydney
Prentice-Hall Canada, Inc., Toronto
Prentice-Hall of India Private Ltd., New Delhi
Prentice-Hall of Japan, Inc., Tokyo
Prentice-Hall of Southeast Asia Pte. Ltd., Singapore
Whitehall Books Limited, Wellington, New Zealand

10   9   8   7   6   5   4   3

Library of Congress Cataloging in Publication Data

Kent, Jack.   The caterpillar and the polliwog.
SUMMARY: Impressed by the proud caterpillar's
boast that she will turn into a butterfly when
she grows up, a polliwog determines to watch the
caterpillar very carefully and turn into a butterfly too.
[1. Caterpillars—Fiction. 2. Tadpoles—
Fiction] I. Title.
PZ7.K414Cat 1979 [E]   82-7533
ISBN 0-13-120469-6   AACR2
ISBN 0-13-120478-5(pbk.)

CURR

Gyt '99

Caterpillars aren't like other folks.
As ducks and hippopotamuses and you and I
get older, we get bigger. Especially
hippopotamuses.

But not caterpillars.

They turn into butterflies.

Turning into something else like that
is not a thing just anybody can do.

Down by the pond there lived a caterpillar
who was very proud of being different.
She bragged about it to her friends.
"When I grow up, I'm going to turn into
something else," she told the snail.

"That's nice," said the snail, who really
didn't care one way or the other.

"When I grow up, I'm going to turn into something else," she told the turtle.

"I don't blame you," said the turtle, who didn't much like wiggly things.

"When I grow up, I'm going to turn into something else," she told the polliwog.

"What fun!" said the polliwog.
"What are you going to turn into?"

But the caterpillar hurried on her way, looking for someone else to tell her secret to.

"I wish *I* could turn into something else when I grow up!" said the polliwog.

"You *will*," said the fish. "*All* polliwogs do."

"What am I going to turn into?" the polliwog asked.

But the fish saw a tasty bug and dashed after it.

"When I grow up,"
said the caterpillar,
who had circled the pond
and was going around
for the second time,
"when I grow up," she
told the polliwog again,
"I'm going to turn
into something else."

"So am *I*!"
said the polliwog.

"*You?!*" The caterpillar was so surprised she almost fell into the pond.

"The fish said so," the polliwog told her. "Fish know things. They go to school."

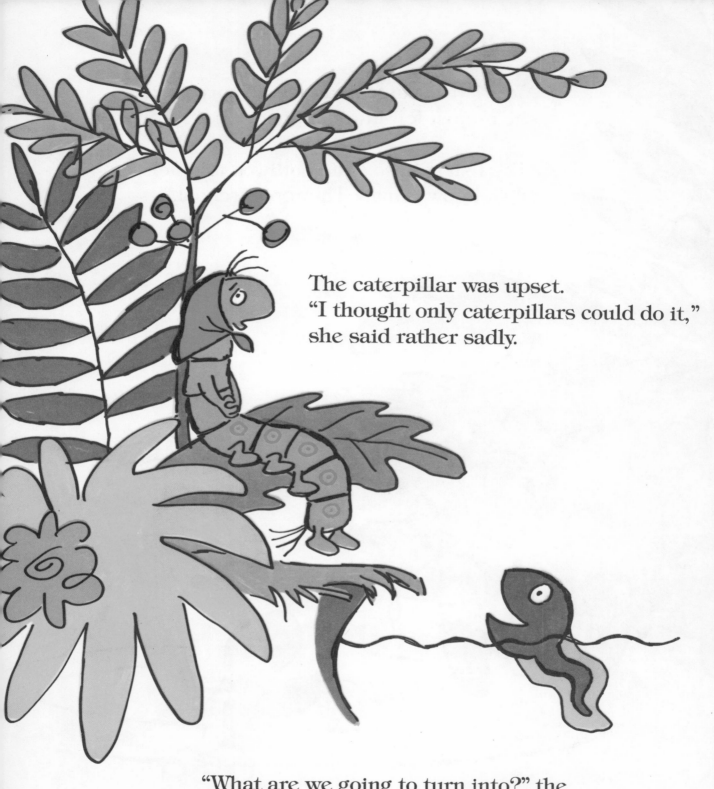

The caterpillar was upset.
"I thought only caterpillars could do it,"
she said rather sadly.

"What are we going to turn into?" the
polliwog asked.

"Well, *I'm* going to turn into a *butterfly!*" said the caterpillar.

"Then I guess I will, too!" the polliwog said happily. "What fun! Let's do it together!"

"All right," the caterpillar agreed, although she would rather have done it alone. "But I get to go first!"

The polliwog didn't mind. He wasn't at all sure how it was done. "I'll watch you," he said.

So when the time came,
the caterpillar started
to spin a cocoon.
"This is the tricky part,"
she said.

The polliwog watched
as the caterpillar spun.
Soon only her head
was uncovered.

"Now I have to close
the lid," she said.
"And when I come out,
I'll be a butterfly."

"Go ahead!" the polliwog said excitedly.
"I want to see you do it!"

"It will take a while," the caterpillar
warned. She started spinning again and was
soon out of sight in the cocoon.

For a long time nothing happened.
But the polliwog was patient.

He watched
and watched
and watched,

for days
and days

and days.

At last there was activity in the cocoon. The end of it opened and, very slowly, the caterpillar climbed out.

Only she wasn't a caterpillar anymore.
She was a *butterfly*! A beautiful yellow
butterfly!

The polliwog was so excited he hopped up
and down with delight!

He *hopped*! Up and down!
Like a *frog*!

"I was so busy
watching *you*," he said,
"I didn't notice what
was happening to *me*!"

"You're a very handsome frog," the butterfly said, as she flew off to try her new wings.

But the frog was puzzled. "I thought I was going to be a butterfly," he said.

A caterpillar wiggled by.
"When I grow up,"
he said proudly to the frog,
"I'm going to turn into
something else!"

But the frog wasn't listening.

He was admiring his
reflection in the water.
"I *am*, you know,
a *very* handsome frog!" he said.